W9-AYR-181

THE MONEY TREE

THE MONEY TREE

SARAH STEWART

Illustrations by DAVID SMALL

FARRAR · STRAUS · GIROUX

SQUARE
FISH

For Edwin and Mary

SQUARE
FISH
An Imprint of Macmillan

Library of Congress catalog card number: 89-46141
ISBN 978-0-374-45295-7

Originally published in the United States by Farrar Straus Giroux
First Square Fish Edition: March 2012
Square Fish logo designed by Filomena Tuosto
mackids.com

13 15 17 19 20 18 16 14 12

LEXILE: AD900L

In January, when Miss McGillicuddy was making a quilt in front of the fire, she noticed an unusual shape outside her living-room window.

In February, as Miss McGillicuddy was looking up from her book, she realized that the new shape was a small tree. "A gift from the birds," she said to herself.

In March, while Miss McGillicuddy was flying her favorite kite, its tail got caught in a limb of the new tree. "What a strange shape," she thought as she tugged.

In April, when Miss McGillicuddy was planting snow peas, she paused and stared at the tree, now covered in the fresh green colors of spring. "How odd," she mused, "that it has grown so very large in such a short time."

In May, as Miss McGillicuddy was making a Maypole for the neighborhood children, she realized, to her great surprise, that the leaves on the tree were not leaf-shaped at all! Being careful not to hurt the tender branches, she gave each child some of the tree's crisp green foliage as a party favor.

In June, while Miss McGillicuddy was gathering a bouquet of roses, parents of the neighborhood children appeared in the yard. When they said they had come to see the strange tree, she invited them to take home a few cuttings.

In July, when Miss
McGillicuddy was picking
cherries in her orchard, the
town officials asked if they
could use some of the
greenery for special projects.
She let them borrow her
ladder—the tree was growing
larger every day—and went
inside to make cherry cobbler.

In August, as Miss McGillicuddy was returning home, she noticed that most of the people carrying bags and baskets away from the tree were perfect strangers! "No matter," she said, "the branches would break from their burden if someone was not picking all the time."

In September, while Miss
McGillicuddy was feeding
the animals, she watched
the crowd around the tree
surging back and forth
beneath the harvest moon.
"Don't they ever rest?"
she asked herself.

In October, when Miss
McGillicuddy was making
faces on her pumpkins, she
realized that the leaves on
the tree were turning yellow
and brown. She sighed
with relief.

In November, as the first
winter storm arrived, Miss
McGillicuddy watched
a few determined strangers
scratching at the snow under
the tree.

In December, Miss
McGillicuddy and the
neighbor boys cut down the
tree. Although the wood was
green and certain to smoke a
little, she didn't mind, for
now she had enough to keep
warm through the coldest
winter.

Miss McGillicuddy gave each boy a loaf of homemade bread, a jar of strawberry jam, and a bouquet of dried flowers. Then she said goodbye, walked toward the warmth of the fire, and smiled to herself.